SIHA TOOSKIN KNOWS

The Sacred Eagle Feather

By Charlene Bearhead and Wilson Bearhead
Illustrated by Chloe Bluebird Mustooch

HIGHWATER
PRESS

Watch for this little plant!
It will grow as you read, and if you need a break,
it marks a good spot for a rest.

When Paul Wahasaypa woke up in the cozy spare bedroom at Mugoshin and Mitoshin's house the sun was shining brightly through the little square window above his bed. He always woke up earlier when he was visiting his grandparents. He loved how their home was not close to any other houses.

One of his favourite things about being out in the country was having the trees all around him. It was so different from his home in the city. Paul liked to "get up with the birds" as Mugoshin always said. Even though he would wake up early, Paul

would always linger in bed with the star blanket pulled up under his chin. He loved the feeling he would get as he lay there listening to the sounds of the birds and the crickets and taking in the smell of the mint tea brewing and the bannock baking.

This morning was no different. As soon as the smell of the bannock got the best of him, he threw back the blankets and jumped out of bed to get dressed.

When Paul got to the kitchen Mugoshin was there making breakfast and setting the dishes out on the table. No matter how early Paul got up he found that Mugoshin had always been up long enough to boil the mint tea, get the bannock in the oven, and wash the dishes. It came as no surprise that she was ready to scramble his eggs when he got up on this day.

Mugoshin looked up from the table and smiled at her sleepy grandson as he entered the kitchen. "Good morning, Mitowjin. Did you have a good sleep?"

"Yeah, I did," Paul answered as he pushed aside some wisps of hair that had come loose from his braid while he was sleeping.

"That's good," Mugoshin responded as she turned back to her work. "I bet you're hungry. Pour yourself some juice while I cook you some eggs. Mitoshin will be back from his walk soon and ready to leave right away." Of course, Mitoshin had already been up, eaten his breakfast, and started his day. Paul always wondered why people said that over the years you get old and tired because his grandparents were always awake and working in the morning before people younger than them.

"Don't you ever sleep in, Mugoshin?" Paul asked as he watched his grandmother washing the dishes and putting the rest of the eggs back in the fridge. "You must be tired because you are always doing something and I never see you sleep."

Mugoshin laughed at her grandson's confusion. "If you want to stay well like Mitoshin and me you need to get up with the sun, Mitowjin. The Creator gives us the daytime to take care of our homes, gather our food, and take care of all of the things necessary for living a good life. We get up with the sun and give thanks to Ade Waka, Ena Makoochay, the plant people, the four-legged people, and the winged people before we start our

own work for the day. They all give of themselves so that we can live."

"If you remember that when you are choosing your food you will also live well. Our traditional foods are medicines for our bodies. We have always eaten the fish, moose, deer, elk, prairie chickens, and the other animals from this area. We eat the strawberries, raspberries, saskatoons, and blueberries that grow here. Ena Makoochay provides the people of the land with all that we need to survive and be healthy."

"It's when we eat too much processed food and fast food that we get sick. Those are not foods from our natural environment. When our people eat too much of that kind of food they get diabetes and other illnesses. That is what makes people tired and low in energy. So you might want to slow down on the bannock, Siha Tooskin," Mugoshin added as she raised her eyebrows. "I know it's delicious but it can be too much of a good thing."

Paul pulled his hand back—he had just been reaching for another piece of bannock when his grandmother's words intercepted him. Paul reflected on Mugoshin's words of wisdom. He knew from experience that she was right about the food. Sometimes after Paul had eaten too much junk food at a birthday party or a movie, he would feel like he was going to be sick and he just wanted to lie down and sleep.

This morning he had enjoyed a good breakfast and he was excited. He didn't know where he was going to go with Mitoshin but it didn't matter. Whenever Paul got to spend time with Mitoshin he always ended up learning something awesome.

Just as Paul was finishing up his last bite of bannock with a bowl of Mugoshin's warmed-up blueberries, the door opened and Mitoshin walked into the kitchen. "You finally awake, old man?" he asked Paul in a teasing tone. "I know you old guys need your rest so I let you sleep while

I went out to feed my horses. Are you just about ready to go?"

Paul knew that he should put his dishes in the sink and help put the juice away like he did at home but he really wanted to get going. As he looked over at Mugoshin she just smiled and pointed to the door with her lips. He knew that was the sign that he was good to go so he hopped off his chair, gave his Mugoshin a big hug and raced out the door after Mitoshin.

When they reached the truck Mitoshin looked down at Paul and asked, "You old enough to drive yet, Siha Tooskin? You can drive if you want to."

Paul laughed as he climbed up into Mitoshin's old green pickup truck and fastened his seat belt. "I would but I don't know where we are going so I'll let you drive this time." Mitoshin and Paul could never pass up an opportunity to tease each other.

"Where *are* we going?" Paul asked as he watched out the window for any hints of what their destination might be.

"Many eagles have been seen flying near the river already this year," Mitoshin explained. "I thought we would drive over to look for some feathers along the banks of the river."

Paul just nodded in acknowledgment of what he had heard as he scanned the sky for eagles. He had seen so many eagle feathers at powwow and ceremonies and in the homes of his relatives, but this was the first time that he had been invited to help gather them. He knew that this was an important responsibility and he was ready to take that on.

When Mitoshin stopped the truck beside the river, Paul didn't jump out and run to get a handful of rocks to skip on the water like he usually did. He knew they were there today with a special purpose in mind. Paul had been taught to respect the Elders, the teachings, and all sacred things. He knew that today was not about playing in the water. If he watched closely and listened carefully to Mitoshin he would learn something very important.

Paul waited for Mitoshin to get out of the truck and then he followed. They began to walk down the riverbank examining the ground closely for eagle feathers. Mitoshin picked up three right away and for each feather that he lifted from the earth he placed a small pile of tobacco on the ground and gave some words of gratitude before

moving on. Paul didn't touch any of the eagle feathers that they found until Mitoshin motioned toward the fourth one that he saw. He held out his tobacco pouch for Paul to take from. Then he motioned toward the feather again. Paul knelt down, placed the tobacco on the ground, and picked up the feather with care. Paul also offered words of thanks to the eagle just as he had heard Mitoshin do.

After some time Mitoshin began to speak. "The eagle flies higher than any other birds. He flies closer to the Creator than any of the winged people. The eagle is very important to our people because the eagle feather carries our words to the Creator. This is a very sacred thing."

Soon Mitoshin stopped walking and turned to Paul. "That is why you must always show respect for eagle feathers, Mitowjin. You must take great care that you don't drop them when you are dancing. You must always handle them with humility and respect."

"It is an honour to have an eagle feather, Mitowjin. Only a few men have the right to trap eagles so that the feathers can be used in ceremonies as well as to protect us and our relations. For the rest of us, we can only gather these feathers from the ground. Though sometimes we find an eagle that has died in the wild, or sometimes we are given eagle feathers by our friends and relatives. To receive such a gift is a great honour. No matter how you acquire an eagle feather you must respect it. You earn the right to keep that feather by doing things for other people. Maybe hunting to provide food to your relatives and community members or gathering wood for the old people. You will also go fasting and follow the traditions, teachings, and protocols as you grow older so that you are worthy of having eagle feathers."

Paul looked up and nodded to show that he had been listening and that he would do as Mitoshin had told him.

As Mitoshin continued walking, Paul followed quietly. He thought about what his grandfather had said.

Paul knew that eagle feathers were sacred. He had looked at Uncle Lenard's eagle fan many times when they were dancing at the powwow and he had hoped that one day he would have one like it. But Paul was confused.

"Mitoshin, if eagles are sacred then why do some of our people kill them for feathers?"

Mitoshin stopped again. He looked out over the river for a few minutes before answering. "Long ago, the four-legged people and the winged people agreed to give their lives so that we could live, take care of our families, practise our ceremonies, and honour the Creator in a good way. The eagle knows that we two-legged ones are the most pitiful of all beings. That is why the eagle helps by giving us his feathers so we can be closer to the Creator."

"Then we use the eagle plumes and feathers for our regalia when we dance. The women wear them in their hair and we wear them on our headdresses. These feathers keep our thoughts and prayers clear and carry them to the Creator as with the feathers on our fans and bustles. The eagle also gives us the feathers to use in our ceremonies, reminding us that we need to keep our ways close to the Creator so that our families will be healthy, strong, and happy. We hang eagle feathers above our doors and above our beds to protect our homes and our children. This is a great gift that the eagle gives to our people. That is why we show great respect and make a tobacco offering when we take the feathers. This is to thank the eagle for his sacred gift."

Paul listened intently to Mitoshin's words. He could picture each of the uses of the eagle feathers that Mitoshin described from his own experience at the powwow, in his home, and with his family. Paul realized that these were things he had never questioned as a small child. He had seen the eagle feathers, knowing by the way his family handled them that they were sacred, but until now, he had not considered the huge sacrifice that the eagle made for the people and how deep their connection with the eagle really was.

Paul recalled that there were certain Men's Traditional dancers who sometimes blew eagle whistles on the drum at powwows. Paul didn't fully understand what it meant but he knew it was very special and a great honour to the drum group who had the eagle whistle blown for them. "Where do the Men's Traditional dancers get their eagle whistle from, Mitoshin?" Paul asked.

"The eagle whistle is made from a bone in the eagle's wing," Mitoshin explained. "The making of an eagle whistle takes great skill and is an important responsibility few have been given."

At this point Mitoshin carried on walking. With so much to consider Paul walked his own path a short distance from Mitoshin just up the riverbank. Paul and Mitoshin looked for feathers until the sun was highest in the sky. They didn't say much more. They just walked and picked up eagle feathers while Paul thought about the words that Mitoshin had shared with him.

In time Mitoshin stopped and looked up at the sun. "I'm getting hungry, Mitowjin. Mugoshin must have our lunch ready by now. We don't want to waste food and it's a long time until supper if we miss lunch so we'd better head back. What about you, old man—are you hungry yet?"

Paul didn't have to be asked twice. According to Ena, Paul was always hungry but this time he could actually feel the rumbling in his stomach. The thought of warm bannock and a big bowl of Mugoshin's delicious stew put a skip in Paul's step. He nodded his agreement with Mitoshin and headed back towards the truck.

Just before they got to the truck Mitoshin took his pouch of tobacco out of his jacket pocket again. He pulled out a clump of tobacco with his right hand and held the pouch out for Paul to do the same. Mitoshin raised the tobacco in one hand and the feathers in the other up high towards the Creator.

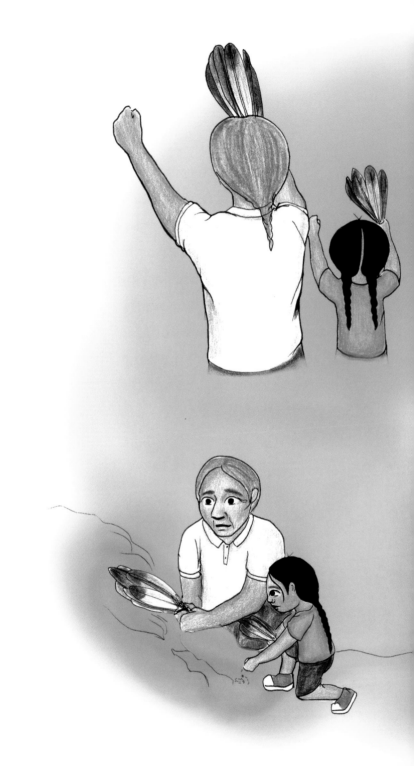

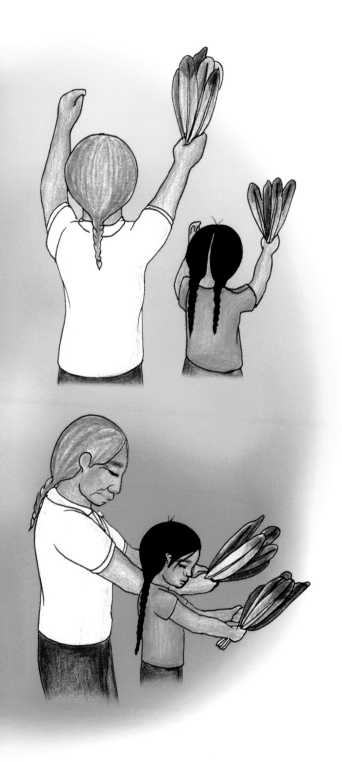

Paul stood silently beside Mitoshin, doing exactly the same: turning to face each direction as Mitoshin offered prayers to the Creator, Ena Makoochay, and the four directions, giving thanks in his Nakota language.

They each placed their tobacco on the ground beside a diamond willow bush. After a short pause, Paul and Mitoshin walked towards the truck in silence. What an amazing morning this had been! As Paul thought about all of the things he had seen and heard in one morning he reached for the handle to open the passenger door. Suddenly Paul heard a loud screeching sound high above them. He and Mitoshin looked up to see a beautiful golden eagle with outstretched wings circling overhead.

"I guess we're not the only ones who are hungry," Mitoshin observed. Paul laughed as they both climbed into the truck. Paul's heart and head were full and soon his stomach would be too.

Glossary

Ade	Dad or father
Ade Waka	Spirit Father or Creator
Ena	Mom or mother
Ena Makoochay	Mother Earth
Mitoshin	Grandfather
Mitowjin	My grandchild
Mugoshin	Grandmother
Siha Tooskin	Little Foot (siha is foot; tooskin is little)
Wahasaypa	Bear head

A note on use of the Nakota language in this book series from Wilson Bearhead:

The Nakota dialect used in this series is the Nakota language as taught to Wilson by his grandmother, Annie Bearhead, and used in Wabamun Lake First Nation. Wilson and Charlene have chosen to spell the Nakota words in this series phonetically as Nakota was never a written language. Any form of written Nakota language that currently exists has been developed in conjunction with linguists who use a Eurocentric construct.

ABOUT THE AUTHORS

Charlene Bearhead is an educator and Indigenous education advocate. She was the first Education Lead for the National Centre for Truth and Reconciliation and the Education Coordinator for the National Inquiry into Missing and Murdered Indigenous Women and Girls. Charlene was recently honoured with the Alumni Award from the University of Alberta and currently serves as the Director of Reconciliation for *Canadian Geographic*. She is a mother and a grandmother who began writing stories to teach her own children as she raised them. Charlene lives near Edmonton, Alberta with her husband Wilson.

Wilson Bearhead, a Nakota Elder and Wabamun Lake First Nation community member in central Alberta (Treaty 6 territory), is the recent recipient of the Canadian Teachers' Federation Indigenous Elder Award. Currently, he is the Elder for Elk Island Public Schools. Wilson's grandmother Annie was a powerful, positive influence in his young life, teaching him all of the lessons that gave him the strength, knowledge, and skills to overcome difficult times and embrace the gifts of life.

ABOUT THE ILLUSTRATOR

Chloe Bluebird Mustooch is from the Alexis Nakoda Sioux Nation of central Alberta, and is a recent graduate of the Emily Carr University of Art + Design. She is a seamstress, beadworker, illustrator, painter, and sculptor. She was raised on the reservation, and was immersed in hunting, gathering, and traditional rituals, and she has also lived in Santa Fe, New Mexico, an area rich in art and urbanity.